HUFF and PUFF
on HALLOWEEN

Warren Publishing House, Inc.

Warren Publishing House, Inc., P.O. Box 2250, Everett, WA, 98203, 1-800-334-4769.

Printed in Hong Kong by Mandarin Offset.
First Edition   10 9 8 7 6 5 4 3 2 1

Warren, Jean
Huff and Puff on Halloween/by Jean Warren; illustrated by Molly Piper; activity illustrations by Marion Ekberg. — 1st ed. — Everett, WA: Warren Publishing House, © 1993.

32 p.:ill.

Activity suggestions included (p. 19-32).

1. Creative activities. 2. Holidays — Handbooks, manuals, etc. 3. Halloween — Handbooks, manuals, etc.

I. Piper, Molly   II. Ekberg, Marion   III. Title

92-62824
ISBN 0-911019-69-3

394.2
(E)

Warren Publishing House, Inc. would like to acknowledge the following activity and song contributors:

Liz Giles, Bellevue, WA
Ellen Javernick, Loveland, CO
Betty Silkunas, Lansdale, PA
Lynne Speaker, Olympia Fields, IL
Bobbie Lee Wagman, Milton, WI
Gail A. Weidner, Tustin, CA

HUFF and PUFF
on HALLOWEEN

By Jean Warren

Illustrated by Molly Piper
Activity Illustrations by Marion Ekberg

Huff and Puff,
One windy night,
Saw some things
That weren't quite right.

First a bat flew
By the moon,
Next came a black cat
On a broom.

They spotted pumpkins
All aglow.
What was going
On below?

While trying to figure out
What they had seen,
They remembered —
Tonight was Halloween!

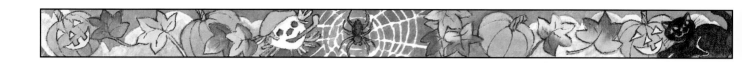

Down below,
Walking by the street,
Were children dressed up
For trick or treat.

"Let's play a trick
On our friends below.
Let's hide the moon
So it won't show."

So off they flew,
Way up high,
Until they reached
The moon in the sky.

They covered it up
With hugs so tight,
That down below
There was no light.

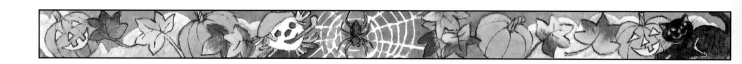

The children were scared,
They started to run,
Suddenly Halloween
Wasn't much fun.

When Huff and Puff looked
Down from the sky,
They saw that the children
Had started to cry.

"Enough of our trick,
Let's give them a treat!"
So they opened their arms
And stretched out their feet.

They spread out so far,
They left holes here and there.
When the children looked up,
They started to stare.

For up in the sky
On that Halloween night,
Was a giant jack-o'-lantern,
Fluffy and white.

Its eyes were all shining,
Its mouth all a-grin.
The children below
Were happy again.

For now the light shown
Back down on the street,
And Huff and Puff's trick
Had turned into a treat!

Halloween Fun

Halloween Songs

Boo to You

Sung to: "Row, Row, Row Your Boat"

Boo-boo-boo to you,
I'll be a ghost tonight.
I will wear a long white sheet
And give you such a fright.

Hee-hee, ha-ha-ha,
Tonight I'll be a clown.
I will wear a big red nose
And dance all through the town.

Yo-ho, ho-ho-ho,
A pirate I will be.
I'll wear a patch across my eye
And sail upon the sea.

Bobbie Lee Wagman
Milton, WI

There Once Was a Pumpkin

Sung to: "I'm a Little Teapot"

There once was a pumpkin
Short and fat,
Alone in the garden
There it sat.
A little girl picked it from the vine,
Took it home and said, "It's mine!"

She carved a funny face
With a great big smile,
Put in a candle
And after a while,
It wasn't a pumpkin short and fat,
It was a jack-o'-lantern, just like that!

Lynne Speaker
Olympia Fields, IL

Trick-or-Treat Holder

 1.

2.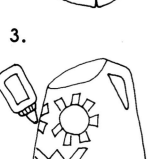

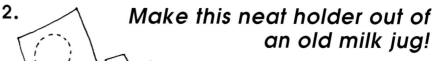
Make this neat holder out of an old milk jug!

3.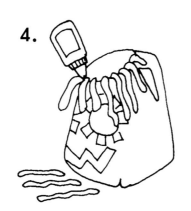

4.

1. Cut the top off a plastic milk jug, leaving the handle on.

2. Cut out two eyes, a nose, and a mouth from colored felt or construction-paper scraps.

3. Glue the eyes, nose and mouth on your jug to make a funny or scary Halloween face.

4. Finish off your holder by gluing yarn pieces around the cut edge for hair.

You Will Need

scissors • a plastic 1-gallon milk jug • colored felt or construction-paper scraps • glue • yarn pieces

For More Fun

• Instead of a milk jug, try decorating a large paper bag or a pillow case.

Halloween Clip-Ups

1.

2.

3.

Decorate your house with bats or other spooky critters!

1. Paint some clothespins black and let them dry.

2. Cut bat wing shapes out of black construction paper.

3. Glue a pair of bat wings to one side of each clothespin.

You Will Need

spring-type clothespins • black paint • a paintbrush • scissors • black construction paper • glue

4. When the glue has dried, clip the bats around the house to surprise your friends and family.

For More Fun

• Instead of using bat wings, glue monster, ghost, or goblin shapes on the clothespins.

• Attach magnetic tape to your Halloween Clip-Ups and use them on the refrigerator to hold notes.

Jack-O'-Lantern Flashlight

1.

2.

3.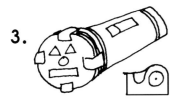

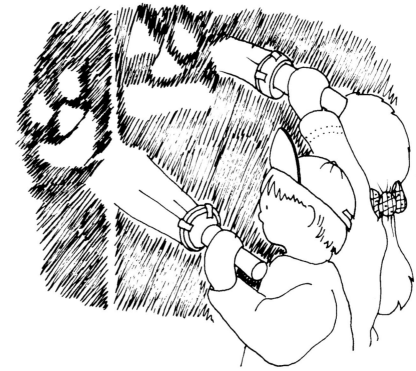

Light up your Halloween with a glowing jack-o'-lantern face!

1. Cut a circle out of orange construction paper. Make sure your circle is large enough to cover the end of a flashlight.

2. Cut a jack-o'-lantern face out of the circle.

3. Tape the circle to the end of a flashlight.

4. Darken the room and shine the jack-o'-lantern face all around.

For More Fun

• Make several Jack-O'-Lantern Flashlights with your friends and race your jack-o'-lantern faces around the walls of a room.

• Make scary, funny and friendly Jack-O'-Lantern Flashlights.

You Will Need
orange construction paper
• a flashlight • scissors • tape

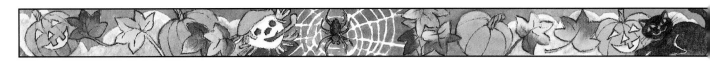

Jiggly Jack-O'-Lantern

1.

2.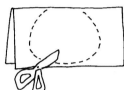

3.

4.

5.

6.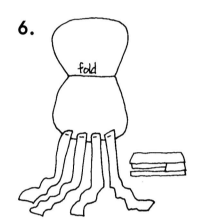

Hang this funny friend outside and watch it jiggle, wiggle, and dance!

3. Cut jack-o'-lantern eyes, nose, and mouth shapes out of black paper and glue them to the front of the pumpkin shape.

1. Fold a piece of heavy orange paper in half.

2. With the fold at the top, cut the orange paper into a pumpkin shape.

4. Cut out a green stem shape and glue it to the pumpkin shape.

5. Cut four or five 2-foot-long strips from a plastic garbage bag.

6. Staple the strips along the bottom inside edges of the pumpkin shape.

7. Staple the pumpkin shape together at the bottom.

You Will Need

a heavy piece of orange paper • scissors • glue • black construction paper • green construction paper • a plastic garbage bag • a stapler

Pumpkin Printing

1.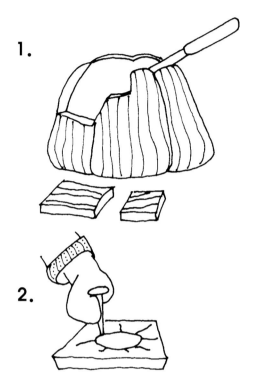

2.

3.

*After Halloween, use your carved
jack-o'-lantern for printing!*

1. Cut a jack-o'-lantern into chunks and scrape off any soft parts.

2. Carve a design on the inside of the pumpkin chunks with a nail.

3. Press the design side of your pumpkin piece onto a stamp pad or a Paint Pad and then onto a piece of paper.

You Will Need

a jack-o'-lantern • a nail • a stamp pad or a Paint Pad • paper

---

Paint Pad

To make your own stamp pad, place folded paper towels in a dish and pour on a little paint.

Gluey Ghost

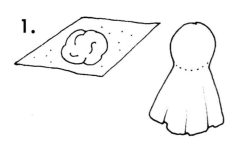

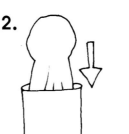

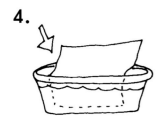

1. Wad a paper towel into a ball and cover it with another paper towel.

2. Stuff the ends of the second towel down into a cardboard tube so that the ball shape is at the top of the tube. This will become the ghost's head.

You Will Need
a cardboard toilet-tissue tube • three white paper towels • glue • water • a black felt-tip marker

Make a stand-up ghost with glue and paper towels!

3. Mix glue with water until you have a thin glue mixture.

4. Dip a third paper towel into the glue mixture and carefully lay it over the ghost's head.

5. Let the ghost dry overnight. It will become very hard.

6. Use a black felt-tip marker to draw eyes on your ghost.

Jack-O'-Lantern Treats

Try these make-ahead treats for your next party!

You'll love these smiling sandwiches!

Jack-O'-Lantern Pizzas

1. Toast English muffin halves.

2. Spread pizza sauce on the English muffins.

3. Sprinkle grated cheese on the muffins.

4. Use olive slices and pepperoni pieces to make jack-o'-lantern faces on your muffins.

5. Ask an adult to help you place the muffins under a broiler for a few minutes before serving.

Jack-O'-Lantern Sandwich

1. Cut a smiling jack-o'-lantern face out of a slice of bread.

2. Spread mayonnaise on another slice of bread.

3. Place a cheese slice on top, and cover it with the "carved" slice of bread.

You Will Need
English muffin halves • pizza sauce • shredded cheddar cheese • olive slices • pepperoni slices

You Will Need
2 slices of bread • 1 slice of American cheese • mayonnaise

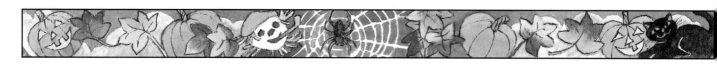

Halloween Brew

Here's a Halloween treat to warm you up!

You Will Need

2 cups apple juice
½ cup orange juice
¼ teaspoon ground cinnamon
2 to 3 whole cloves

1. Mix all ingredients together.

2. Ask an adult to help you cook the brew on low for 20 minutes.

3. Remove the cloves and cool the brew a bit before serving.

For More Fun

• Make a Halloween straw for sipping your brew! Just attach two stickers back to back near one end of a straw.

Orange-Pumpkin Pudding

Ghosts and goblins love this treat!

You Will Need

4 slices whole-wheat bread

½ cup milk

½ cup orange juice

¼ cup apple-juice concentrate

2 eggs

1 banana

2 teaspoons cinnamon

1 cup canned pumpkin

Dash salt

1. Tear bread slices into small pieces and ask an adult to help you crumble them in a blender.

2. Place the bread crumbs in a large bowl.

3. Ask an adult to help you mix the remaining ingredients in a blender.

4. Add the blended mixture to the bread crumbs.

5. Stir and pour into a buttered baking dish.

6. Bake for 50 minutes at 350°F.

7. Serve warm.

Roasted Pumpkin Seeds

1.

After carving your jack-o'-lantern, save the seeds to make this yummy Halloween snack!

2.

3.

4.

1. Rinse pumpkin seeds and remove the pulp.

2. Pat the seeds dry with a towel.

3. Mix the seeds with melted margarine and Worcestershire sauce.

4. Spread the seeds out on a cookie sheet and sprinkle them lightly with salt.

5. Bake at 350°F until the seeds are brown and crispy.

You Will Need

Pumpkin seeds from 1 pumpkin

2 tablespoons melted margarine

Dash Worcestershire sauce

Salt

A Note to Parents and Teachers

The activities in this book have been written so that children in first, second, and third-grades can follow most of the directions with minimal adult help.

The activities are also appropriate for 3- to 5-year-old children, who can easily do the activities with your help.

You may wish to extend the story even farther by discussing clouds and all the shapes they can form, or by talking about being afraid, or even by making your own Halloween learning games (such as matching cards with jack-o'-lantern faces).

Children learn so much better when they can express their ideas and feelings through age-appropriate activities. We know you'll enjoy seeing your children's eyes light up when you extend a story with related activities.

Huff and Puff on Halloween

Sung to: "Yankee Doodle"

Huff and Puff went out to play

One dark and windy night.

They saw a bat fly 'cross the moon,

It was a scary sight.

Down below the pumpkins glowed,

What a strange scene.

Then they saw the children out—

Tonight was Halloween!

Huff and Puff loved Halloween

They loved to trick then treat.

First they scared all of the kids

Out walking by the street.

Then they planned a big surprise

Way up oh so high,

A giant jack-o'-lantern

Smiling in the sky.

Jean Warren

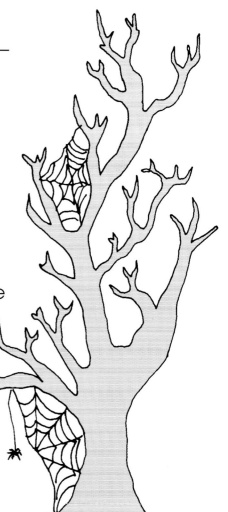